Hair rising, Heir raising, Erasing

By Cordelia Malthere

Dedication

To my favourite dreamer of all,
Dad,
André Nicolas
RIP
2013
Your cheerful optimism made me believe in dreams.

To a dream maker who never ceased dreaming marvels
till his end,
To a talented musician and writer,
Martin Simpkin
RIP
2013
Your constant belief in making dreams happen,
Your encouragements made me pursue mine.

To those influential Father figure's,
I have to add,
Tyn-Tyn
:)
Still alive and kicking
You are the dream architect that gives dreams their
structures.
XXX

To Chelsea,
:)
You are an essential part of the dream,
Helping to make it happen.

This story is an homage
To
Charles Dickens
'A Christmas Carol'

My inspiration for this story,
Is
A dark whimsical dream,
In which I woke up from the dead opening my own coffin.
By morning,
The first lines of 'Hair rising, Heir Raising, Erasing'
Were created.

-Well, well, well, I'll be damned, we can't sleep in peace anymore. What is that cacophony all about?

A skeletal hand pushed open its coffin lid grumpily and a bewildered dishevelled skull appeared, peering outside full of suspicion.

As the cadaver saw others stepping outside of their graves, he realised that something was definitely, disturbingly going on, and he pestered,

-Blast! I will be damned for sure this time around, for it is the bloody apocalypse, and the rising of the bloody dead! Well, I will be better off playing dead and ignoring it all happened, I am sure everything will eventually vanish like a bad dream.

The skeleton cowardly nestled back within the padded security of his coffin, closing back his lid with great care, hoping, praying that none had noticed him.

A loud shrieking voice however saluted him eagerly,

-If it is not Sir Abraham Wilton-Cough, I will be damned and dusted! Hello, how are you keeping after all those years? I didn't seen you turn up at last year's event. Some are harder to rise than others they say. It all depends upon the heart. You have got a very fearsome look upon your face, you do recognise me, don't you Mr Wilton-Cough?

The cadaver rolled his eyes with pure annoyance, muttering between his teeth, before lifting his coffin lid with a sense of bothered obligation, and faking a welcoming smile,

-Yes, be damned and dusted, bloody neighbour! Blowing my cover up as usual, old bat, some never change with time.

Then announced out loud,

-How could I honestly forget you, dear widow Bates, my neighbour for twenty years, now that I am going to be damned with you? I can swear upon my empty grave that you haven't changed at all. Now, tell me all, as you always knew everything about what was going on, see, I remember the old days. Tea in your grave, or whiskey in mine?

The widow readjusted her bonnet, and swinging shakily from one skeletal hip to the other, giving her most cadaverous smile,

-Abraham! Flatterer, truly I shed much weight since. I am now as light as a feather and no more strangling corset needed, see. No need to bring my smelling salts to wake me up from any fainting spell, all I need nowadays is them, playing of their instruments with love to rise and dance all night. Your grave is much too formal to be entertaining, even with a glass of whiskey or a whole flask, for that matter. I am going where things do happen.

The old skeleton of Wilton Cough rose from his grave, and standing with a whimsical smile before it, pointed at it proudly, and argued,

-What is wrong with my tomb, pray? Show me yours, woman, of the world you were, hey, living within two rooms your entire life while I had a house and owned half of the old town. Show me the grave that charity bestowed upon your corpse. Let's compare the material, the wood, the state of my degraded body to yours. I still have hair and clothes, after so many years, what are the gold letters saying intelligibly? Year, 1837 AD. I would bet yours can't be read, erased and eroded with time. I am the great descendant, eleventh removed from the founder of our town, the notorious Noah M Wilton, and the glorious son of Terah Wilton Cough. What can you say for yourself ignorant woman?

The ancient skeletal woman, grabbed a pair of very old spectacles hidden within her bonnet, and putting them before her eyes sockets, advanced,

-Yes, it is very grand to have a name, the names of your forefathers and dates showing up after so many years in gold upon the marble, I must applaud at that I suppose but they forgot to put something else, something meaningful about you, a eulogy. Did you leave nothing to be talked about between your birth date and the last one? Come and see my grave...

Abraham followed her, very annoyed, and pestered,

-You do read, Bates? Since when?

The old cadaver ran before him, and exhibited her tombstone with some pride, before answering,

  -Since I had a husband in the army, and it would be useful for me to read the newspaper, to know or guess half of what was going on in the world... Look, here is my eulogy: 'here, lay the sweetest and dearest of souls, Mrs Amelia Bates, born Elroy, February 1801, the adoptive mother of many orphans of Wilton Town, the biggest, largest and richest heart known in town until it passed away, blessed by all in August 1876. Look at the freshly cut flowers upon my tomb, my adopted children prospered and their offspring are still paying me respect. Yes, materially, you outdo me, Abraham, but spiritually I do not think so. But I have a confession to make. My blessings started with your mistake, ours, and they never stopped from pouring in from its blessed conception.

Wilton Cough covered the sides of his skull with his bony fingers and cried out loud,

  -Hell and damnation! Upon my bones! Have you got no respect for the dead? I do not do mistakes. Never did! Your conception must be, has to be miraculous. There must be a mistake, for Christ's sake!

The widow Bates shook her head negatively and assured,

-Oh, no Abraham, there was no mistake or rather a big one on our parts. We were drunk, off our heads, and all night I did ride your old bone, and dried it out. In the morning, I found myself alone, naked and a dirty handkerchief by my bed with your name on it, and the tell-tale smell of its stains. I could not remember anything at all, and had only vague and blurry flashes of things and something not memorable at all. I had to piece together what did go on, and the more I found out that it was very questionable, regrettable and unmistakable that it did happen, I had to think out of my way and wit to get away with it. My shame came more that it was done the night of the funeral of my poor husband Harry. This was indeed disrespectful of the dead. But I came to terms with my guilt, by seeing it in a clearer, concise and sobered way. First, I was so distressed at his death, crying rivers, that as a kind neighbour for once you must have decided to give me your shoulder, and obviously things led from one thing to another, and if alcohol is great to alleviate grief, it also tends to alleviate grey matters from the brain cells, so it is explicable. Second, I was alone for five long years when poor Harry passed away, far away, so hormonal biology obliging, being only human, a little touching and all my cravings were released at once, if it was another shoulder than your one, I am pretty sure the same thing would have happened, maybe a little bit more memorable even, so it is explainable. Third the ensuing miraculous conception had to be well hidden for me not to be stoned by my not so kind neighbours and parish. Upon the blessed, kind and forgiving advice of Father Odell, I became fat with grief: the poor widow Bates couldn't stop eating and after the birth I kept cushions under my dresses to still be the fat Bates. It worked until one day, a couple of years later, I didn't have to use the pillow ploy as I was by then really fat. The night of her birth, I left my baby girl on my own doorsteps and miraculously found her the following morning in a little basket, nicely wrapped up with a note, and of course, I adopted her. Everyone believed me so much that my doorsteps became the receptacle of other little unwanted ones, from all over Wilton Town. Now, as I wasn't going to throw the first stone at myself, I forgave myself for my mistakes and errors, and then I became the mother hen blessed with all the tiny mistakes and errors of other women and men. As my days of loneliness ended, my days of blessings truly started by raising all the unwanted children. If you follow me you will meet them.

Old Abraham looked around a little alarmed, concerned that the widow's avowal may have been heard by anyone else, and scolded her,

  -Right, charming, do you happen to know what apocalypse means, bloody woman? With all the dead rising from their graves, it is far from the perfect time to confide cheerfully how bad we were. Now, pray why would I want to meet the unwanted ones, the mistakes, the errors of all? I had two of my very own children and I was never inclined to find out how worrisome and tiresome they became after my death. Informed presently that I had a third one, a girl, doesn't stir my bones ecstatically with joy especially knowing how naughty and bad her mother was. Let me rest in peace and go on your way.

Mrs Bates gave him a wicked smile and teased,

 -Dear old devil you! I swear that you are scared. Shivering all over like that. Your bones are clacketing uncontrollably. I could bet that you have lots on your mind.

The cadaver denied it at once, wrapping his skeletal arms protectively against his chest to make it stop its frightful shaking,

 -I am no devil and a Wilton-Cough has never ever been scared of anything. Besides I have nothing on my conscience for I have none left, dear old mindless you! Look!

To convince Amelia, Abraham removed his skull and showed it to her scrutiny, adding strongly, speaking from his bony hands,

 -See, very empty indeed, there is no black nor grey matter to bother me at all. It was all munched happily away by maggots ages ago. What bothers me right now is that apocalyptic racket going on.

   -Come you must regret one thing or two for we are all far from perfect and only human after all. Besides making mistakes is part of life's learning curve. I have done a fair few in my time. The best mistake of all was our daughter, for example, which taught me never to regret some of my errors.

Putting his head back upon his corpse, the cadaver stamped his feet, pestering,

   -I do not regret anything, I am as perfect as all the Wiltons and the Coughs assembled. My life was an example of no mistakes made at all. Do not insist upon the subject, woman! I do not want to listen to your bloody mistake either for I deny it, once and for all.

Grabbing his hand, and tugging it repetitively, in order to make Abraham follow her, Amelia Bates insisted nonetheless, so much so that the skeletal arm of her neighbour stayed within her hand, dislocating itself,

   -Come and see who you want to ignore before you deny anything. Maybe then you will admit that she is the perfect pride of the Wilton-Cough. Let's go to her mausoleum.

Rolling his eyeballs in his eye sockets full of desperation and outrage, Wilton-Cough cried out at the sight of his severed arm,

-Murder! Someone's killing me! Take her away, she is a grave robber, she is stealing my bones. Arrest her!

Then he stopped all of a sudden as he repeated, dumbfounded,

-Mausoleum?

-Oups! That's yours... For sure, your old bones are far easier to come now when handled. Let me put it back where it belongs. I did not mean to walk away with it, all I want is to walk with you to her grave, the finest in the town.

As the widow Bates helped to replace his arm, Wilton-Cough repeated, his interest peaked,

-The finest?

She nodded positively and confirmed,

-Oh yes, the very finest. You, who know your finery at the tip of your fingers will be able to assess it. Our little mistake did very well indeed for herself. Although I can confirm to you that she had humble beginnings. Like me she was acquainted with poverty very well indeed, and like me she never let it break her good spirits.

Starting to follow the old Amelia, Abraham mentioned,

-Surely my very legitimate two boys who went to the best schools did better than her. Maybe they are not buried here because they made something of themselves elsewhere which means we do not have an appropriate comparison.

-On the contrary, we do and can make a comparison. Follow me, I will show you their graves. For one of them, we have to come out of the cemetery for his body was not allowed on consecrated ground. For the other, it is an entirely different matter altogether.

Almost running down the hilly graveyard, the widow arrived to a Gothic ironed gate within the surrounding crumbling walls. As she opened it, it emitted a ghastly rusty longish squeal which chilled Abraham Wilton-Cough following her to his very last bone. However he dared to ask when the skeletal arm of Amelia went to nestle itself within his,

-Why was he buried elsewhere than the cemetery? Of which of my two sons are we talking about?

As they walked along a small foggy path by a dark forest, Bates replied,

-It's Jo. He had an ugly life and end.

-You mean Josiah Wilton-Cough, my younger one. How did he end?

-I am afraid to announce that he was hanged.

Staring in front of him at the darkness, Abraham sighed deeply then repeated somewhat startled,

-Hanged. Hanged? How?

Making a gesture in the air mimicking a garrotte squeezing a neck, the widow answered,

-With a big rope and all, publicly, in the market place. It was one of the last big condemnations in Wilton Town.

Shaking his head in disbelief, Wilton-Cough took his top hat off and held it upon his cadaverous chest, confiding full of sadness,

-It cannot be. Josiah was a little poncey boy that played piano all day long. He would not have hurt a fly, that's why I sent him to boarding school to toughen him up. What happened?

Fastening the ribbon of her bonnet, Mrs Bates felt strangely swallowed back in her gossiping time when she first broke the news to one of her neighbours, as she started,

-Well, brace yourself, for it is somewhat very sad indeed. I remember little Josiah hiding in his mother's skirt wherever she went. She dotted on that boy like no other. Angela Wilton-Cough used to invite us for tea parties where Josiah was put very much on show playing all the nice tunes he had learnt on the big piano. He could have been a great pianist if you hadn't intervened strongly and discouraged greatly his growing passion. He loved to endear himself in the company of women. He felt safe there. Removed from his loving home, forced to quit his tender years, Josiah didn't understand why his older brother could be at a school near home while he had to go far away when even weekends had to be spent there and only holidays brought him back to his loving mother. The sweet boy was bullied like no other in that school. The fear of displeasing you prevented him to disclose the bad treatment he received from teachers and pupils alike. He kept silent until you passed away. Josiah was about twelve then.

Abraham seeing ghosts gliding silently, sweeping past them slowly, sadly commented,

   -Angela was spoiling the boy into a weakling. What was a father supposed to do?

   -Maybe understanding your child would have helped better than imposing your own will upon him. Do you realise that humans have been given free will, Abraham? Therefore by suppressing the tender will in young Josiah, you took the freedom from him allowed to all humans. We need everyone to build a world, even in the animal kingdom, the ant's colony has roles for different individuals. Try to force a Queen ant to be a worker and she may not fit the bill at all, fail miserably and die away having wasted her life by peer pressure. Let her be a Queen, see her thrive and in consequence, the entire colony in her wake. What wrong could have Josiah done being nurtured into the pianist he wanted to be? Listen can you hear him play? He plays for the lost souls now. Yes, he is handling notes of a different kind than the ones you wanted him to deal with as a banker, but you have to admit his ones are divine and yours just paper that rule too many hearts to become calculating machines devoid of humanity.

Wilton-Cough listening attentively could hear a very famous tune played so well that it grabbed his absent guts. He closed his eyes for a split second, before opening them again, glowing with glee, as he said,

　-It is the 'Toccata' of Bach. Indeed he is handling the piece very well. But think about it, woman, he would not have made much money to scrape a living as a church organist, now would he? I understand what you are implicating but life means also a concern for all its requirements: feeding, bedding, roof and so on. One cannot be too fanciful about those matters. I aimed to give him the ability to earn what could buy him anything.

The widow sighing deeply, stated,

　-Indeed you did. He learnt to toughen up, to handle the paper notes so much so that sweet Josiah became tough Jo, a shadow of himself for the rest of his life. I can tell you what money cannot buy for you my dear old Abraham, although you always did seem contented by money, it is happiness.

Arriving at a crossroad, Amelia showed him a weathered single blue slate stone face down marking it at it's middle and asked,

   -Help me turn this one around. This is Josiah's gravestone.

As the stone was lifted, Wilton-Cough took notice of its simple acknowledgement of his son, by the words 'Jo W-C' which looked badly carved. No dates were to be seen and no comments either. He asked sorrow rising within his chest,

   -What happened for him to end up this way? What did he do? Did a child write his name on the stone for the handwriting to be so awkward?

Putting back the stone, Mrs Bates confided,

   -No one was allowed to mark his grave this is why it was turned upside down. However one of the girls he looked after, the only one that could write, came back in the midst of the night to make sure Jo would not be forgotten. He was very loved by all his girls, even after his dreadful death they never had a bad word to say about him.

Abraham smiled all of a sudden full of hopes,

-A philanthropist! Like you, Amelia! I knew that child could not be that bad, he helped raising others.

Amelia, fiddling with her bonnet, a little embarrassed to break more news, corrected,

-Well no, it was very unlike what I did. How can I explain? His girls were big girls, well not fat, no, fit most of them, like in a painting of Renoir, and of the gorgeous kind. Well, you see they were adults and he made a business out of them. He picked up all the poor destitute prostitutes living in the streets of Wilton Town and gave them a roof and protection so they could carry on their business safely... I mean he only charged them rent at very minimal prices, fed them and even clothed them, I heard from very reliable sources. They never mentioned him as a whorehouse owner but as an open minded landlord with strong arms who would kick out violent pricks and save the girls from harm. It was philanthropy but not as we know it. He never judged a girl, he just offered them a protective hand and home. His kindness became so renowned that he attracted many to him from all over the land. Although his rent was low, he earned money by keeping a bar for the visitors where he played every night the piano, keeping all waiting happily and in check, I was told.

Putting his hands on his skull faking covering his ears,

the cadaver pestered,

-The shame, the utter bitter shame and disappointment.

Taking the defence of his son, Mrs Bates scolded,

-Well, shame that you did not give a single penny of inheritance to your younger son. Shame that you made his elder brother the sole heir of your fortune leaving your wife and Josiah to his charity. What shame do you carry, having failed to provide for the bare necessities of your poor widow Angela? Your eldest followed your example to the letter. He grew no heart, no compassion and as soon as he inherited, sold your home and left his mother and brother in the streets to fend for themselves. Their sudden destitution was harrowing to witness, and it was prostitutes that gave them charity at first, sharing their meagre meals with them. Then a well to do Call Girl took pity on the begging Angela and Jo. She proposed your wife to become her maid and little Jo who had started to learn the street's laws with his fists to be her bodyguard. A few years later when the Call Girl passed away she gave all she had and her home to her two servants. She wanted to make sure they would be alright after she was gone, for by then she considered them as her own family. This is to put you to shame, Wilton-Cough, that Lady did what you didn't do to your family. You were a bitter disappointment to your loyal Angela, and as a father to your youngest son.

Old Abraham was taken aback as no one dared to contradict him during his life let alone tell him off. He saw the woman grab his hand and lead him out of the beaten track, inside the dark forest full of ghostly laments. He asked full of fear,

-Where are we heading, Mrs Bates? I do not like the idea of getting lost in the middle of nowhere.

-We are going in the middle of the forest. The little clearing there is haunted by your son Jo and his girls. You will have a chance to meet him and tell him why you decided not to provide for his mother and himself in your last will.

Shaking like a leaf the cadaver replied,

-I do not like the sound of that idea either! Let's return to the cemetery at once.

-No, Abraham, it is the night of the dead and you will face the music. Everyone is going through it as they rise, I am afraid.

Surprised at the sudden strength of the widow Bates, Abraham Wilton-Cough followed, scared that it was a judgement night, one that he dreaded already. Ghosts were lurking in the dark by trees which sounded alive in the wind. The autumnal forest floor gave the whisper of its rusty leaves at their every step until they reached the small clearing. Bathed in moonlight, the grass shining with dew, the place was swept by swirling and dancing shadows, who cried and laughed all at once. They twirled gracefully around the most amazing piano that our two cadavers never saw during their times as living humans. The twisted and terrifying blend of tail piano and church organ gave the instrument a sound eerily perfect. At its ivory and ebony clavier, playing away tune after tune after tune was Josiah, oblivious of his surroundings, swallowed by his own music.

Almost stuttering Abraham whispered to Amelia,

-I think, I think it is best to leave him lost in his, his melodies and not to disturb him whatsoever.

-Fiddlesticks! Let's meet him! If I didn't know you better, I would swear that you are slightly scared of him: your son is intimidating you, at long last. Tables do turn around once in a while frighteningly so. Do you remember dragging his young hand to that boarding school, to his new intimidating Head Master? Do you remember the constant beat of the ruler that teacher played upon his own hands while welcoming his new pupil? That ruler beat your son's palms to a pulp one day to that very same rhythm that is filling the air now. I think you cannot go back, Jo is acknowledging your presence by his musical welcome... Do you remember what you said to him in front of that Head Master? Let me refresh your memory and tell you exactly the same: Come on, man up!

As the first notes of the Symphony No. 5 of Beethoven resounded, the cadaver shivered, his hand dragged by the widow until he stood by the formidable piano confronted by a ghost as formidable as his instrument. Abraham wished to run away, hide away deep into his grave, yet his fear paralysed his every bone to a frozen stand still. Taking his hat off, humbly, he tried to venture to break the distressing silence between him and the fearsome ghost that kept playing,

-Beethoven, powerful sounds. Maybe if they are associated to a punitive and painful past, we should start afresh with something else, something more cheerful, you and me...

The ghost nodded with a sarcastic smile as he started another tune which made all the shadows lift their arms towards the night sky as if they aimed to grab the moon and the shimmering stars. The feminine ghosts started walking in a slow and sad procession, sobbing all around the piano getting closer and closer to Abraham Wilton-Cough at each turn. The cadaver touched ever so slightly by a shadow shivered all over and jumped sideways and argued,

-Yes, that tune may have put your old tyrannical father to the grave and give you a smile but it is hardly a new start, rather than an end now isn't it? I do like the 'Funeral March' of Chopin hence why I chose it for my funeral but you struggled after that sad event to make ends meet, you and your mum I have been told. It hardly brings any comfort to my dead bones and yours, now does it? Play something else, something that means new beginnings. Rise above your sorrow Josiah. Please, talk to me my son.

Slamming closed fists upon his clavier, the ghost gave an incendiary glance at his father as he said sternly,

  -I have no father. Mine passed away, dead and buried, he is best forgotten. He was a miserable man who made a point of ignoring my mum and I's mere existence. It past the point of no return. It was sealed with his grave. What is left are only memories of a dreadful individual who should rot in his tomb undisturbed for the peace and sake of everyone else.

Chastised, a silent Wilton-Cough saw his son starting another tune with a gusto which did not disguise the distaste he had for the presence of his father by his terrifying instrument. As the notes of Mussorgsky's 'Night on Bald Mountain' rose powerfully in the air, ghosts from the forest glided in great numbers into the strangely glowing clearing. Growing uncomfortable, the cadaver made a last attempt at communicating with Josiah, who did not seem to pay attention to him anymore throughout his speech,

  -I guess my explanations will be ignored, but I have to tell you the truth. First you were very much my son all the way through, but I felt embarrassed by you. I truly did not understand you while your mother did, irritating me by doing so. I made all the wrong decisions then, from removing you from her to take you to that infamous boarding school and from discouraging you to be the musical artist you were clearly born to be. Second I trusted my values over any values anyone would have, my will over anyone else's will to be the one, the only one and the best to have. I not only disregarded your wishes, I tormented your free will to subdue it to follow my rules, and the glimpse of an idea I wanted you to be. My dreams saw you, my second son, as an astute and strong banker with a head for figures, able to build his own path with gold bars. I thought the school would help to shape you to fit my dreams for you. This was the plan, to keep you away from my nightmares as I saw you being the star of the show within a drawing room full of ladies, sipping their teas, praising you endlessly, comparing you to what they knew about music and the Sunday Church organist who hardly scrapped a living together. Third, yes I did take you away from my will and your mother just as well. I followed my own dream for you when I did it, and buried your very own dream for good at the same time. I followed the wise words of my financial adviser, my best friend, who told me to not spread my wealth out but to focus it on the basket who could withhold it and keep it consequential. Your mother was a leaking basket who would have indulged everyone in the neighbourhood daily with tea parties. Encouraged by her, you would have become another leaking basket, splashing my wealth on fancy dashing clothes and state of the art instruments only to amaze everyone at the Sunday service with only applause for reward. Fourth, I believed your brother would have made you finish school for I left a fund to that effect. By 18, you would have known how to fend the world adequately. But also I never imagined for one second he would have made your mother and yourself homeless. I trusted that he would look after you sensibly enough, not indulge you but just take care of you two. I have just learnt, it was not the case, and I am ever so sorry for it.

The fists of Jo fell heavily upon the ivory keys again finishing chillingly his last tune as he rose from his stool and ordered,

-Never entrust someone to do the good you had the power to do yourself. Do not start the blame game and wash your dirty hands and dark heart away. I heard enough from that vile soul, drag him away back to the dust where he belongs.

Pointing to Abraham before sitting back upon his stool and playing another piece, the 4th movement of Dvorak's Symphony no. 9, the ghost stated almost in a whisper,

-For you, old man. May your love of hate and your hate to love be dusted from this Earth.

The ghosts grabbed Abraham Wilton-Cough's arms and legs and dragged his old bones away from his son, his music and his words. Terrified, petrified, ashamed, the old soul stayed silent throughout its ordeal, which took him back to where he had come from in the first place. Thrown back into his grave without one ounce of regard was enough for Abraham to bite the dust with his every tooth remaining in his skeletal jaw. Laying there, almost numb, the corpse acknowledged however,

-Fair point. Taken far too late to be remedied upon. It hurts my every bone very much so right now.

He heard a good knocking on his coffin's lid and the now dreaded high pitched voice of Amelia Bates,

-Mr Wilton-Cough? Mr Wilton-Cough? Abraham, are you alright?

Grumpily mimicking her within his grave, the upside-down cadaver stated,

-Does it look like I am alright? I have been dragged by an army of ghosts, for Christ's sake! Go away and let me rest in peace in one piece. You heard him, none of my children has the desire to meet me in this after-life, not that I had a particular interest or need to meet them either.

Pushing open the lid, the widow stood there with a very disapproving look upon her face, her skeletal arms folded across her chest, as she scolded,

-Now, Mr Wilton-Cough, you must rise above those feelings especially on a night like this one.

-No, it's a racket out there. Beside my own son said that I should not be disturbed for the sake of every one.

Then Abraham added with deep sadness in his voice,

-Was I that despicable? I'd better do as he told me and wait to turn to dust.

Presenting her hand with a look full of kindness, Amelia Bates ordered,

-Come with me. Let's find out together.

Despite shaking his head negatively, the cadaver took the hand presented and let himself be guided. The widow trotted along a cemetery path which look very much disused and unattended so much so that Abraham was worrying about where it led. His wondering mind was soon answered as a giant pit lay before them in the middle of which a large rickety table was surrounded by many decrepit skeletons chatting away happily. In the midst of them, he recognised the small and slender Angela Wilton-Cough. She seemed like she used to be during her life the heart of the party. However all her smiles disappeared at once only to be replaced by a shiver when she noticed she was observed by an unwelcome visitor. Angela came to them, opening her arms to the widow, she embraced her warmly and invited,

-Amelia, what a pleasure to see you. I can't help noticing that you are on guide duty again, but I hope you can stay a little and share a cup of tea with us. It's a remarkably mild night for the season, don't you think. Apart for that cold breeze, it almost still feels like summertime.

Putting her bonnet in a more elegant fashion, Mrs Bates told with false shyness,

-I would love a cup of your delicious brew to warm my old bones, but I feel very under dressed to join your elegant tea party Mrs Wilton-Cough.

Looking at the desolated area and for him the evident abject poverty of all the guests, Abraham pestered for himself in a low voice,

-Flattery. Who are you kidding? A miserable bunch blabbering about whose the worst for wear and has the most worn out bones of them all.

Mrs Bates scolded him secretively at once giving him a serious elbow jab which dislocated his forearm,

-Abraham, this is not called flattery, it is called kindness and charity. Angela always prided herself in offering generous and heart-warming tea parties for all in the neighbourhood. It is not her fault that she is now holding them from her pauper's mass burial ditch. Now, come along and behave yourself.

As he saw that his wife had already returned to her table full of guests without a word to offer him, he asked Amelia in a whisper,

-I do not think Angie is seeing me, Mrs Bates, or she must not recognise me at all.

The old widow straddling by his sides corrected,

-Oh no, make no mistake, Abraham, Mrs Wilton-Cough knows you are here and sees you alright that's why all her bones went all shaky and shivery with sheer repulsion or it might be fear, or it might be a bit of both. After all like I, she is acquainted with your old bone and like I do, it might be a vision she wishes to forget. Now, let's put that arm of yours back together. That's better. I do not know why I am so brutal tonight, I am usually an excellent guide. Did you ever touch your wife in a brutal manner? For that would explain it, for the moves of a guide are the first punishing ones you do encounter once risen.

Feeling very uncomfortable with his pride abated tenfold, Wilton-Cough took his top hat within his hands, clutching the brim, and started turning it around full of uncertainties within his long bony fingers, the rim held tight against his chest as he defended himself,

-I, upon my very own dishevelled skull, never raised my arms against Angie, my finger, yes, I did indeed, and my tone many times. It doesn't make me the worst husband now, does it?

-Well, the combination of everything you did to that woman put you on the scale of the bad ones. First, staring right in front of you, is the fact that she ended up in a pauper's grave and that you could have prevented this from happening. Josiah would have, if only he would not have been convicted of the murder of one of the rich customers frequenting his establishment who was trying to strangle one of his girls after battering her. After the good left punch he gave, the man fell, his head smashing against a false marble statue full of lead sealing his departing fate to the after-life. Protective Jo was hung for the death of that horrible man who had killed a fair few women during his life. But that man was so rich that he bought lawyers and almost the law to remain unpunished. The street law that Jo learnt got him in the end, but it ultimately cost your son's life as well. With his untimely death, poor Angela was left struggling again at a grand old age. She passed away in the bitter winter of 1866, the very same day as Mr Thomas Love Peacock. She was frozen to death as she slept that night on the church's steps of Wilton Town where she begged for a living since her son's death and their inherited home was seized by the state. She met a very sad end, Abraham. If only you would have cared a little more, it would have been entirely different.

Arriving at the table, Abraham saw plenty of old corpses ready to shift for the widow and one offering his own place to Amelia Bates most gallantly, yet none offered a seat to him. The fuss was all about making sure Amelia was made comfortable while he was totally and utterly ignored. Silently digesting the news of what happened to his wife at the end of her life, Wilton-Cough felt that his presence was sincerely not welcome at all and understood why. Standing almost still, behind the seat of Mrs Bates, Abraham felt ever so small, the very size of his pea sized shrunken dried heart. He stayed there not wanting to disturb the jovial and convivial tea ceremony, and just watched. From the eclectic variety of tea pots and crockery he realised that the party was very much a communal effort.

His wife invited with a lovely smile,

   -Would you care to try this beautiful addition to my tea collection, Mrs Bates? It is called Lady Grey, a black tea scented with bergamot, orange and lemon peel, and a touch of lavender.

   -I would with great pleasure, Mrs Wilton-Cough. Have you heard the news in your neck of the cemetery?

Pouring the tea in a cracked porcelain cup, and presenting it to Amelia, Angela asked full of curiosity,

   -News, no we haven't had any news at all since you last came to pay us a visit a couple of weeks ago. What is happening in the big wide world?

-Well, I heard from very reliable sources that tonight was the night where all the vile and cruel people the world has carried would finally rise like the others but also that they would suffer and be punished very severely.

Going to sit at the head of the table, Angela commented like if she had been struck by enlightenment,

-That would explain everything. We saw the famous bank robber running away from his ghostly victims and later it was the notorious rapist of Wilton Town.

A very unsettled Abraham looked at his bony hands in shame realising that if he did rise that very evening, having never rose before that put him straight in the same ranks as criminals. He could not gaze at his wife anymore, nor any others, feeling deeply saddened and ashamed by the news. With a bowed head, he heard Mrs Bates replying,

-I got it from good authority that those dead are going to be all pulled apart publicly before sun rise. That promises to be a spectacle. Are you coming to see the big judgement?

Shaking her head negatively, looking straight at her husband Angela answered,

-No, there is no one that matters to me and is of consequential importance for me to attend.

Trembling behind the chair of Amelia, Abraham felt his chest constricting, remembering how he had been with his wife during his life. Unpleasant, overbearing, full of authority, and demeaning were words whistling in his ears along with a nagging disloyal, which kept repeating itself over and over again. He whispered full of dread to Mrs Bates,

-Does Angie know about our mistake?

Turning to him the widow replied out loud in a tone that did not allow any secrecy whatsoever,

-Of course she knows, like everyone else does that you have been infidel to your wife, that you were cruel enough one day to tell her that if a Wilton-Cough had not a duty to have an heir and carry his lineage you would never have married her. We all know how she was put upon day in and out. You did not have to lift your arms, Abraham not at all, your voice was enough to deliver a daily mental battering. As if that wasn't enough you ignored her existence totally in your will. You reap what you sow. In death Angela will never acknowledge you.

Chastised in front of all, Abraham felt like crying of sorrow, yet his eye sockets remained burningly bone dry as he saw Angela sipping her tea peacefully, like if he was not there, standing helplessly. He broke his imposed silence, came shakily by his wife and knelt by her seat,

33

-I know it is far too late to say it. I know it is just going to be ignored. But I want you to know that I am ever so sorry for everything, everything I ever said or did to you. Please, accept my sincere apologies. I am not proud of what I did, Angie, especially to you. I would offer you all my honest tears if my skeleton could cry for I did love you. I remember the first time I saw your enchanting smile, it was at the tea party of my aunt Josephine and her very words to me: 'whatever you do Abraham, do not fall in love with the Italian shop keeper's daughter.' I disobeyed and did the right opposite, for I could not forget the beautiful raven black curls, the deep blue eyes like the ocean to dive into, the yellow buttercup dress spreading around you like the rays of the sun. Anytime I see you somewhere, it is like gasping a big breath of fresh air, like seeing the sun in spring after a long winter, like feeling finally vibrantly warm inside. I am sorry to have loved you badly, jealously. I was never a lover of parties because I was always scared to lose my dazzling little sunshine in there. For I never understood why you would take a shine to me, for I was average at everything apart from Mathematics. I guessed as I was not a very dashing prince it was only my name that bought your hand and attention to me. My own doubts about myself turned me into a bitter man. I kept my rays of sunshine boxed up in my home wanting no one to see them yet you opened the box and the tea parties started. I couldn't object to them, but when Josiah made them even more popular by his musical talent, I did the unthinkable and intervened. Now all I can see is having made the terrible mistake of separating my very own family apart, breaking all its love and warmth. Angie, I have very deep regrets and I just want you to know that. Here, take this for all it is worth, it belonged to you all the way, or throw it far from you and trample it. I am ever so sorry for everything and definitely not proud of what I have done.

Grabbing his dry heart from his cadaverous chest, Abraham pulled it, and presented it before his wife upon the table, before rising to his feet silently and left the pit with his sadness increasing at his every step as no one commented upon his sorrowful speech but carried on the conversation like it never took place. He could hear Mrs Bates commenting joyfully,

  -What a delicious brew! You can indeed feel the bitter sharpness of the lemon in it.

  -The Tang of the orange peel makes all the difference. If someone had created that tea back in the day, I would have fallen in love with him. More biscuits, Amelia?

Devastated, lonely, Abraham Wilton-Cough walked towards his grave lost in his sad thoughts when he saw his son's ghost Josiah followed by his ghostly girls upon the same wild path heading towards his mother's pauper's ditch. Moving sideways to let the ghosts past, the skeleton stood there silently hoping not to be recognised, nor noticed for he remembered what Mrs Bates had said about the dead being dismantled. His wishes were not granted as he saw the imposing figure of Jo stopping right by him and asking,

-Do I know you from somewhere, skeleton? Lift your skull a little so I can see you properly under the moonlight.

Frightened Abraham obeyed taking a good glance at his son as he replied, keeping his hat close to his chest,

-You do know me, Josiah. I am your father, the one that is very sorry for everything he did or almost.

Smiling cruelly to him, Jo crossed his strong muscled shadowy arms upon his chest, repeating like if he was tasting the very word within his lips,

-Almost... What could you possibly not be sorry for my dear father? The Authorities are rounding up all the souls that woke up tonight by the statue of Noah M Wilton, I suggest you go there with no further ado. They are playing the greatest game of pick a bone to ever been seen. Guess what your name appeared on the very list of contestants that made it through to being pulled apart. How does it feel?

Gulping, his throat the driest it ever was, the cadaver answered,

-Terrible. I feel terrible. If I could dig the ground underneath me and hide in shame, I would, Jo. I just saw and realised what became of your sweet mother. Your words are still resonating within my mind: I should have done what I could for you two when I had the power to do so and use my own heart rather than let it fail you in such a way and passing my duty of you two to your brother. I am ever so sorry for what happened to you and my dear Angie. She is not going to my debone-ing for I do not exist anymore for her. I do not blame her. Will you come? The sight of my demise might give you your own back a little. Let me tell you that the very first time I held you in my arms and saw the same blue eyes as Angela staring at me, I was far from sorry for my actions then, I was very proud of the result of one to say the least. Let's not stop you on your way any longer. I am going to be cleared and dusted from anyone's path soon, son, do not worry. My three last words to you are: I am sorry.

Before he could answer anything Jo saw the skeleton of his father leaving, his expression ever so forlorn, heading now towards the main town rather than his own grave. Grabbing the hand of the twirling ghost of one of his girls, Josiah kissed it with a knowing wink and a smirk, and waved farewell to his father,

  -See you gutted later, old man. I will care to come to your demise.

Catching a last glimpse of his son, Abraham moved along the path, deeply sighing, and started to talk to himself to try to quench his incredible sadness,

-Yes, see you later. I thought you would appreciate to see me gutted somehow, my now little big fruit of my loins. Awesome ghost, you are, very...very scary. Look, I am somehow moving towards any of the directions you pointed to me tonight. Oh my, oh my, when I dreaded a slow dusting alone in my grave, now I am walking towards worse. What have I done? What have I done? Oh my, Oh my. It would be such a lovely evening to rise truly if I had not cocked up so beautifully my life. It is warm like an Indian summer. The moonlight is just, just mesmerising, glowing upon everything: the path, the graves and their robbers. Robbers, thieves, my grave, they are doing my grave among many... Oi!

Waving his arms erratically Wilton-Cough went running forward in an incentive to protect all graves and especially his own one. He tried the very fearsome and ghostly 'Ouuuuh, ouuuuh' and the more immediate ' schoouuuh, schouuuuh' but the effect was not what he expected. No one flew away from him and his skeletal sight, instead he faced the grave robber that was doing his very grave pointing a machine gun at him. Lifting his arms up surrendering at once, Abraham pleaded,

-Right, I give up! Kill me once more. You'd better be a sharp shooter though to not miss a rib between all those cavities.

The grisly gunman shouted astonished as he shot away at the skeleton,

-Dad! What a surprise! How are you doing?

-Apart from being shot at, son, I guess I am fine, dead and all. Honestly, what does it look like when my grave is being robbed by my own child and my carcass is flying into little pieces? Did I not give you enough with my whole inheritance for you to loot my tomb? Now, have the decency to answer me and cease your fire.

Grinning wildly Zachary Wilton-Cough laughed out,

-The problem with those machine guns is how to stop them after they start. I still need to work that one out.

Firing everywhere and nowhere in particular trying to find a way to stop his gun, the very tall and pale Zach caused more injuries to his father, his robbing friends and himself. Seeing a piece of his son's brain flying away from his skull, Abraham decided to intervene, leaping forward and offering his scolding assistance,

-The thing that makes it start and stop is called the trigger, you bloody nincompoop! Just take your finger off from it, release it before making more damage around you. You don't want to lose more of your brain cells, do you, as you seem to not have enough already?

Doing what Abraham told, his son gave his father his most beautiful smile which displayed a set of very yellow and very long inhuman teeth, as he swore,

-Gosh! That's a clever trick to know. Where did you learn that one, dad? Before, I just dropped the gun until it stopped like the others.

Wilton-Cough looking around saw two of the 'others' crawling on the ground, bleeding badly, injured and begging for help by the graves they were robbing. He smiled for himself that his cease fire call had such an unexpected result among the robbers because of the sheer ignorance of one of them. However he was stupefied by the monstrous physicality of the robbers. His son should have been dead by now, not only from shooting at himself in a willy nilly fashion, but deceased over a hundred years ago. Yet he was standing in the graveyard with bleeding pale blue flesh attached to him. Something was up which deeply unsettled Abraham, who dared to enquire,

-As a bank director, owning a pistol was a necessity, although it did not save me from being shot by a bank robber and dying from a single bullet hours later. Your companions look very unwell, mind you it is not surprising after being pierced through and through like colanders, Zach and you, you look very different... Somewhat taller, very blue with very pointy teeth... What happened to you?

Trying to fix up the part of his flapping scalp, Zachary winked at his father with a cocky smirk as he answered,

40

-I am not too worried for them two, for the less we are the more we feast. Apart for that missing bit of brain now don't you think I look dashing and very well preserved, dad? I will let you into our little secret to great longevity: we eat people dead or alive, the fresher the better.

Stepping away from his son, seized by an uncontrollable shiver, Abraham was in total disarray. It dawned on him that Zachary Wilton-Cough went through his tomb: was he looking to eat his very own father? He pointed to his grave shakily then to himself repetitively a few times wanting explanations, demanding,

-Do I truly look like a happy meal to you?

Turning around his father ever so slowly, considering him as meat for the grab, making Abraham tremble of fright doing so, Zachary finally stated,

-Not as very well conserved as I expected, I am afraid. I thought your money would have bought a decent coffin with tin like quality attached to it. Yet I am very much mistaken, you are pretty much rotten all over. Your bones might still make perfect toothpicks for dirty nachos.

The terrifying Zach went to pick up a piece of Abraham's rib that laid flat at his feet from the shooting, and put it in his mouth to illustrate his point. Then he showed a silver flask of whiskey, waving it slightly to his old man, before commenting with his brightest grin, and licking his purple lips,

-When I thought this little silver baby with it's vintage golden content was the most precious thing I could grab from your grave, I come to the realisation that your good old bones taste like cheese straws so full of marrow they are.

Calling out his companions at once, Zachary Wilton-Cough shouted, pointing at his father,

-Guys! Snack time! Cheese straw bones down here!

Forgetting his intentions to pick up all his pieces of shattered bones within his top hat at once, Abraham legged it out of there as fast as he could. He could not say he was running for his life for his one was lost so many years ago. He did not know where to go nor who would give him shelter. He ruled out rushing back to his wife's ditch and ruining her tea party with greedy bone snatchers. He ruled out losing Zachary in the ghastly and ghostly woods of his good son Jo' for he knew he was by his mum dutifully paying her visits after all those years. His only hope was the 'Pick a Bone' game and joining it as fast as he could. As he ran fast and forward, the old threatened Wilton-Cough bashed himself upon the statue of his ancestor: Noah M Wilton, the founding father of Wilton Town.

Catching his breath by the effigy, the cadaver was ever

so ready to give up. Zachary, who he had always believed to be his best son turned out to be his worst one, and a flesh eating monster, that was a revelation he could not cope with especially since his bones were about to be swallowed by his son like delicious straws. This must be his last straw, he thought. However a strong voice and hand recalled him,

-Abraham, stand up and face everything. You are one of mine hence strong. On your feet now.

Lifting his eye sockets up, Wilton-Cough saw the statue of Noah by him, holding his shoulder with his solid brass fingers glowing in the night like a beacon. Lifting himself up the old skeleton finally dared to look around him at the very place of his own promised demise. Lifting his head up Abraham acknowledged his ancestor by an apology,

-I am sorry to not have fulfilled your footsteps very well. I am considered to be one of the worst souls, a miserable one. My very bones are up for the grab. I must join those lost Beings hurdled by those armed guards for sadly I am one of them.

Seizing the chin of the skeleton, the statue of Noah revealed,

-This very town was founded by eating our own dead. This is what we had to do to survive. Some of our descendants are since plagued to become ghouls. The fate of Zachary is not your fault, it is entirely mine. Let me deal with your bone suckers. Join the others and wait for your own judgement.

Doing as he was told, Abraham Wilton-Cough saw the colossal brass statue of his ancestor stepping down from its base and brandishing his huge axe against the incoming ghouls. It resounded like the clashes of the titans with gunshots hitting metal and the vibrant noise of the battle axe against flesh and bones. The living dead were literally hacked off Wilton Town by its very founding father.

When the head of his favourite son hit the ground, a very sad and bitterly disappointed Abraham reached the crowd of criminals awaiting their sentencing. He felt utterly ashamed of himself as he considered the lot of skeletons surrounding him. Suddenly a sharp tug dragging his hand shook him out of his morose thoughts along with that pestering, persisting and now familiar voice of Mrs Bates,

  -Abraham, here you are! I thought I lost you for good. Come with me, we still have plenty of time before your turn at the strike of three thirteen am precisely.

Wilton-Cough followed her finger which pointed at the magnificent clock tower of the town hall and the actual time: quarter past two. He barely had an hour left before meeting his fate. He smiled piteously to the widow as he stated,

-Somehow I cannot bear the dreaded wait any longer. I am utterly sorry for what I have done and very ready to pay for it. How do you happen to know the hour of my punishment Mrs Bates?

Winking at him with great cheerfulness, the old Amelia readjusted her bonnet before enjoining Abraham to follow her,

-Because I made a point to know everything. For every matter that matters are close to my heart. Now there is only one way to beat fate my dear Abraham, so do not be defeated before it is all over for you. You have one hour to go and sixty minutes to make something out of them. The clock is ticking, the countdown has started. Come with me and keep listening to your heartbeat.

With a quick glance at his hollow chest, knowing he had given that little shrunken dried nugget of a heart to his wife Angela, Abraham didn't find the courage to disappoint Mrs Bates and her running enthusiasm by telling her that it might be difficult to listen to a heart when it was a totally absent organ and just followed the footsteps of the widow without argument and almost eagerness.

Yet when they reached the trendiest part of the old town, Amelia considered him with an amused grin upon her face, as if she had read his thoughts all the while,

-My poor Abraham, where have you been all along? Missing bones and all, looking the worse for wear. In fact you are just the picture perfect of having taken a very serious battering. Who are the culprits, pray? Could you have done better and spread about your entire heart to all at all times. It would have prevented so much heartache for others and you, don't you think? Every good beating count to correct and redress a situation. The heart is the key so take heart and keep courage. We all acknowledged that you did bestow a golden nugget of one like everyone after all. Make it physical again and listen to its power. Face the concept and embrace it before it is too late.

Utterly lost within thousands of thoughts bursting in his spirit like tiny bubbles of hope listening to the blabbering Bates, Abraham begged,

-Amelia, where are you leading me?

-To face your errors, all of them, and fight and rectify all you can.

The cadaver considering his appalling state again rose his skeletal eyebrow ridges at the sheer hope and restlessness of the widow, thinking she had just gone bonkers over time. However as they stopped at the steps of a great mausoleum made of pink marble, he remembered that Mrs Bates gave him a posthumous daughter. Having met a terrifying ghost and an even more unsettling ghoul as his very beyond the grave sons,

46

he could not help being awfully worried about the occasion he finally had to meet yet another of his dreaded spawn. He made small talk to give him reassurance,

-Beautiful marble, I must admit Mrs Bates. The tones are almost flesh like, and the exquisite subtlety of those veins running through it are simply remarkable. I can only bow and concede that what you said at the start of this evening was right all along. I wish my bank was decorated with such stone slabs, it would have made a great statement in my time rather than my well-treaded upon solid oak planks. Where do those come from?

A beaming Bates climbed the steps, almost joyfully like if she was a little bird, all dancing and singing,

-It all comes from China, the Fujian province. Do you remember refusing bank accounts to two refugees from that area a couple of weeks before your death? Well, it was Cabrel Town who welcomed them with open arms, their banks bestowed those beautiful marble floorings a quarter of a century later and are still there to be seen, shinning like a statement to embrace anyone with a loving exchange.

Biting his lips Abraham swore,

-Blast, am I accumulating mistakes upon mistakes, Mrs Bates? If I remember right your very father was an Irish man who struggled thoroughly as he arrived in the town to raise his ever growing family. How many little Elroy were you in the end? Twelve, thirteen? How many of you did make it?

Amelia replied sighing,

 -With the stamina and hard work of my father, we almost all made it but one. We could have been twelve but were eleven for mum passed away giving birth to a little baby boy who did not survive, giving his last breath a couple of hours later. We did have nothing but the strength of love to keep us going then. All the Elroy children were assets to Wilton Town. The two eldest sons created a small business together using their crafty hands creating from scratch Victorian furniture like no others. The two eldest daughters became another small partnership and held a little shop around the corner selling their dress making skills to the neighbourhood. I became good old widow Bates myself, the mother of many unwanted little ones in Wilton Town, helping them grow up to account for themselves and take a place with pride and honour due to their own skills and merit. The others did equally well in their own right. Returning the same question to you, Abraham, how did you make it?

Reaching the top of the stairs, Wilton-Cough looked around proudly feeling on top of the world however replied in all honesty,

 -I always thought I did very well for myself. I owned the entire town or almost until I decided to get partners.

I came from a very favourable background, the Wilton associated to the Cough and made the most of it. I created the first bank of Wilton Town. I am proud of that achievement yet, yet, I failed to use my heart so many times that I believe I did not do as good as I always thought I did. I wish I saw the consequences of my actions as I was doing them, for now I am far from being proud of them. I have been heartless to my own family so many times that it kills me. I was neither a good husband nor a good father, it pains me to admit.

Joining him at the top, Mrs Bates commented with satisfaction,

   -Well, well, now there Abraham, everyone makes mistakes, to admit them makes you a better person. To eat humble pie when the cookie crumbles takes courage. Tonight you took that first step and I am frankly proud of you. It is still an uphill fight but you are making very decent progress. Here, meet our mistake. I called her Abigail. Isn't she gorgeous?

With a sudden deep shyness the skeleton stared at the being in front of him who had an ethereal beauty about her, literally glowing from her every pore. He could not believe his eyes of how resplendent his daughter was. She was no monster child either for she bestowed a set of wings as white as snow. Bewildered as if it was too good to be true, Wilton-Cough asked in a stutter,

   -Is, is she, Abi-b-bigail, truly an angel?

49

The mother could not help having the proudest smile as she nodded positively and answered,

-She is. Can you call her a mistake now?

Looking from the cocky grin of the widow to the peaceful smile of the winged creature they had created together, Abraham took sheepishly his hat off before admitting,

-I cannot. I said many things during my life and after-life which I was sure of with the up most overruling certainty, but I am now lost for words and truly regret a great many of them uttered that did more harm and hurt to everybody without regard nor consideration.

Mrs Bates took Abraham by the hand then exhibited to him the surrounding marble walls, ceiling and floor of the mausoleum enjoining him to read the golden scriptures on all of them, parading the deeds of the result of their common infidelities,

-She was the brightest child in her school. Look at those medals and diplomas. She became the first female doctor in Wilton Town let alone one of the entire country. She financed her studies nursing at the hospital. She was a very hardworking girl, and courageous like no other. Abi volunteered to help during many wars, and earned tremendous respect with everyone doing so. These are her war achievements, don't read it all, I can resume it for you: she mended many soldiers back to health and gave them back spirit and hope. It is during that time that our busy bee met her future husband, a rather dashing yet rather wounded captain. It was love at first sight. He became a much loved president of our country and she was his first lady. This is when her charity work started in full swing up until her death. Abigail was inspirational and many followed her footsteps. She spread her love and care to many. This is how she earned her wings and became an angel.

Wilton-Cough was mesmerised by it all, knowing that his girl had very humble beginnings yet made it to be a president's wife but most importantly a personality that all would remember with affection and great respect. She was a true descendant of Noah M Wilton who created Wilton Town out of utter wilderness with his broad axe, he thought unlike him. He would never be remembered in such a way. His own grave proved it for its lack of a eulogy. Abraham sighed deeply, for even poor Mrs Bates had the nicest eulogy he ever saw, putting him in the shadows of shame. He turned to Amelia and Abigail, uttering in a heartfelt plea,

-I wish I would have made a difference to others like you both clearly did. But all I can brag about is that my very own family wants to see me dismembered or swallowed in their stomachs, down and dusted, and that the love of my life doesn't want to hear about me whatsoever. My biggest mistake was to not care for them as I should have. I wish it was otherwise.

Abigail, spreading her white wings majestically before her father took his bony hands within hers then whispered before pushing him into the deep hollow that was her own grave within the mausoleum,

-It is quarter to three. Your wish is granted, Soul, however you have only minutes to repair what you can.

Falling into the deep darkness, Wilton-Cough swore out loud,

-It must be my demise, it must be my own end, the end of it all. Oh Lord! I hope I won't meet you in the other end.

His eyes blinking into the dim bedroom, Abraham thrust himself upwards only to fall back upon the pillows. The doctor by his bed side reassured the devastated and tired Angela,

-It will soon be over. He is just coming back from his delirious fever. I am afraid Ma'am this is the time when you should say your farewells to your husband. I will call for the priest. Do you want me to call your sons by your sides, Mrs Wilton-Cough?

From the deepness of his pillows, Abraham's voice rose at once answering for his wife, almost breathless,

-I do want my sons to be there. Please Angie, do me

one last favour, my darling.

Angela standing up at once, looked upon her dying
husband astounded, not by him pulling it through to
consciousness somehow but by the simple little magic
word he never used to order her about the house being
so softly said. Holding the pale hand of the dying banker,
she replied,

 -Anything, just ask my Ab. Doc, call my sons to come
into the room. They are anxiously waiting for any news
in the living room.

When the Doctor departed, Wilton-Cough realised he
was about to die. He was on his very own bed back from
a profound delirium. A quick glance to his blood tainted
bed sheets, and a very deep bloody burgundy bandage
surrounding his guts confirmed his worst fears, truly he
would pass away. Was his journey beyond the grave just
a fever induced trip, a delirious dream? Clearly he was
back in his cosy bedroom and well looked after by all.
When he took a quick look at the Swiss cuckoo clock he
hated so much, the wedding present of Auntie
Josephine, that Angela loved so much so that she
wanted it to be in their bedroom, he noticed that it was
quarter to three and could not help shivering in a panic,

 -Angie, grab the key in the left pocket of my jacket,
then go to the reproduction of Watteau's drawing of the
hatted widow by your dressing table, behind it you will
find my safe. Keep everything in there for yourself just

burn the only letter for that is my very will, as fast as you can. Then get me a witness. Our neighbour will do, Mrs Bates. I want to write my entire will again, and I have not got a lot of time to do so.

His wife obeyed as his two sons arrived within the bedroom. Seventeen year old Zachary looked very self-secure with a confident smile upon him at all times even when his very own father was about to pass away. While twelve year old Josiah stood very shyly within the room staying by the door ready to step outside, as if unwanted. Abraham encouraged,

  -Come here you two. I have something important to tell you.

When Zachary stepped forward, Josiah stayed still upon his spot terrified at the sight of his dying father. Feeling every physical pain within his body, warning him of his countdown, Wilton-Cough tried once more desperately to call his youngest son by his bedside,

  -Come my Jo. I am very sorry to be in such a state before you. I am also very sorry to have taken you far away from home. There's no more boarding school for you, for mum will need you right by her side, and I do count on you to give her all the support she needs. I heard that they mistreated you at that school, which pained me greatly. Now, you mustn't stop educating yourself for having met bad teachers. For mum will have the task to find you a couple of tutors, one for your general education and one of music.

Dropping the letter in the fire, Angela could not retain her surprise at the decision of her husband who had preached an entirely different stance all along with their little Josiah,

-But I thought you did not want to encourage the boys into any fruitless artistic pursuits, Abraham.

Wilton-Cough watching his last will burn to ashes offered a sorrowful smile to his wife and children,

-Yes, I did say plenty of things along those lines, but the fact and the truth are as I am at my last minutes, that I must admit that I was entirely wrong many times for I have no right to impose upon you to live your very own lives a certain way that suits me and no others. The three of you are free to live your lives as you desire, to follow your own dreams. Make the most of every minute for they do count and never forget that there is only one rule to be respected...

A painful burst of cough stopped his words as Abraham tried to catch his breath, with the desperate hope that it was not his last. The burning sensation throughout his body however confirmed to him that it must probably be otherwise. Josiah ran to the bed and poured water for his father, offering the glass with trembling hands, asking in a whisper,

-What is the rule, Pa?

Grateful of the kind gesture of his little boy, Wilton-Cough drank his eyes glowing with tears then touching his own chest and tapping it gently continued,

-It is to listen to your heart, to use it and to love one another. Just don't follow in my footsteps when you grow up, Josiah nor you Zach for I was not the nicest nor the kindest man. You need to follow your heart and be good individuals respectful and caring. If you both promise me that you will try your hardest to do so then at least I will depart with more peace within my own regretting heart.

As his sons obeyed mimicking their father's gesture, their hands upon their hearts, making the solemn vow, the doctor returned within the room accompanied by the priest and Mrs Bates. In a night dress covered by a large black woollen shawl that had clear tell-tale signs of being slowly eaten away by moths, the widow readjusted her bonnet announcing,

-Oh dear, oh dear, oh dear, my poor Angela. When we all thought that Mr Wilton-Cough would last forever and bury us all, he jumped in front of a bank robber to protect his customers from harm.

Abraham looking at his neighbour could not help a rising smirk upon his lips as he confessed sarcastically out loud,

-Well it was more protecting them but most importantly my money. A live customer is an asset and future profit in my eyes, Mrs Bates. Of course, it would have worked that way perfectly for a long time if the bastard didn't shoot me in the guts.

The priest intervened at the bitterness of the comments,

-Abraham, maybe it would be best for your sons to step away now before you confess everything to everyone. Have you said your farewells to them?

Chastised, Wilton-Cough took a quick glance at the definitely round belly of Mrs Bates despite all her care to camouflage it. He closed his eyes almost in despair, for this was one fact he was not aware of up until his feverish nightmare. What if everything he dreamt was true, real and would come to pass? The man reopened his crying eyes to face his family as he pleaded,

-Zach, Jo, give your old man a kiss and I beg you to remember what I said for your own sake for I love you both very dearly. Josiah, you are a talented pianist and do not let anyone ever tell you otherwise. Be my boy and find it in yourself to forgive me if you can. You will make me the proudest father if you play the 'Marche funébre' of Chopin for my funeral. Zachary, I made the mistake of spoiling you. Forget whatever I taught you for it will get you nowhere but in a state of true sorrow at the end of it all. Start from scratch with the education of your heart: just do what I haven't, care and respect.

Boys, it's with great sadness that I have to say goodbye to you two.

The tearful sons embraced their father before leaving the room together, Zach wrapping his arm around the shoulders of his younger brother. When they closed the door behind them, Abraham was left with a decision to make, the one to reveal his deepest shame and embarrassment to his beloved wife or not. Heartbreakingly torn apart, the husband remained totally silent considering his dilemma. On one hand, he only strayed once, just one single night, one when he was not sober at all, one moment he so deeply regretted that it bothered him endlessly ever since it was committed. However hard he had tried to forget it or ignore it, it pestered his troubled conscience in the depth of his death bed and his feverish dreams. Yet it took only his weakness of a few minutes to put Mrs Bates into trouble herself with her own reputation at stake. On the other hand, he had been a very jealous and domineering husband, preventing his wife to go out by all sort of excuses in the book, plaguing her by his constant lack of trust. He had not been the most kind and loving partner, she ever met on the contrary. Will she be able to forgive that kind of revelation let alone understand it? Will she hate him for eternity, having been the very tyrant who could not be trusted?

When he felt her gentle hand within his, met her deeply worried blue eyes, asking with tender anxiety,

-Are you still with us, my Ab?

Wilton-Cough nodded positively reaching to a decision finally,

-I am. My Angie, what I am about to tell you pains me deeply. You already know that I wasn't the perfect husband and far from it, with only a redeeming glow of my wealth and our position in society. I have been an arse with you all the while when I was desperately in love with your beautiful self. Angie, you do mean the world to me and forget every harsh word I said to you for they were just lies and done in the heat of the moment. The one that I would only marry to have an heir was pure hurtful bullshit for you made my day every day, and that is the truth. I am ashamed to say that I was a bastard to you, for I did the unthinkable once, the night of the funeral of Mr Bates when you decided to invite all back to our home, when I took Mrs Bates back to hers afterwards in such a drunken state that she could barely walk by herself. When I was myself not with it at all. I am afraid that I cannot ignore the fact any longer that at the mere sight of her ever growing belly that she is with child, and that is very much the result of my inebriated error. I am ever so sorry for it, Mrs Wilton-Cough because you were very much so the only woman I ever loved in my entire life. I mean it and it hurts thoroughly to admit that I done you wrong. Forgive me if you can but I will understand if you don't.

Angela squeezing the fingers of her husband together

told him in her own personal confession,

-My Ab, Amelia and I are bosom friends: we have no secrets between each other. Rest in peace for I already knew everything, the predicament and I did forgive you both within my heart. If Dr Valdi and Father Odell keep to their sworn word, your confession will remain our secret forever. We will all look after your little mistake with the up most care when it comes to the world with bright colourful crying cheeks. Father Odell came up with a bright plan to make it all acceptable and covered up beautifully.

Finally finding back his smile, Abraham queried,

-Does it involve Mrs Bates eating many cakes downtrodden by grief?

When his wife, the doctor, his confessor and the widow reacted by a common stunned:

-Yes, it does.

Wilton-Cough could not help his confident grin upon his face despite his entrails creating a launching and excruciating pain from within. The cuckoo clock announced three am soundly enough for the man to be utterly worried once more. If everything was right, it was his very last hour and he had only thirteen minutes left. He cried out in an emergency call,

-Grab a pen, fetch paper, may all of you bear witness to my last will.

As Angela kept firmly his hand within hers, Abraham dictated his wishes to the widow Bates who was dutifully writing his every word. When the long arm of the clock reached the thirteenth minute of the hour, it was all over, for Abraham Wilton-Cough had nothing left to say to the entire world having given his last breath. His tearful wife closed his eyelids tenderly and kissed his lips full of sorrow herself, confessing softly,

-I forgot to tell you that I loved you for your proud guts, not your wealth, my Ab, and now I love you for yourself, for eternity.

The End.

**Hair Rising, Heir Raising, Erasing.
By Cordelia Malthere.**

A vibrant beyond the grave tale which will chill your bones while warming your heart. When the deadly serious is delightfully hilarious, you will know you have just been acquainted with Abraham Wilton-Cough. His skeletal hand will drag you from grave to grave, under the moonlight of the night where many dead are rising... Could it be the apocalypse?

By the same author:

Finding It-666: The Beast
Book 1 of the teenage Antichrist years.

Born on the 06/06/1996 in London, the young It is a sweet sixteen supernatural Being of a special kind, one meant to bring the end of the human world: the Beast incarnated, the Antichrist.
Fall 2012, the Beast was found. From the deep darkness of her hole, she is raised up to the light. From her closed caged below a pentagram made of blood, she is freed. The human who found her, Walter Workmaster, is a firm atheist, a private investigator and former human rights lawyer who becomes her staunch advocate. Adopting the lost It, the man released her to his world to make her face humanity and unknowingly much more... The advent of the Beast has started. Step one, she is found.

Coming Soon:

**The Compendium of Characters of
Cordelia Malthere.**

Take a guided tour in the It-666's saga and the Author's fantastic stories' world. Switch gears from Earth to Hell to the unknown... Meet the characters, their pasts, their presents, and maybe their futures... This Codex is the ultimate companion to Cordelia Malthere's universes.